CHAPTER ONE

A werelion prowled the library shelves, pacing amongst the rows. The werelion aspect wasn't a huge surprise considering the town was filled with them. From the sheriff to the school principal, members of Penelope Little's pride held many positions. Including Penny herself as the town librarian.

So, a furball roaming the stacks was a familiar occurrence. Especially on Wednesday after the kindergarten reading circle rampaged through the space.

The only problem was this particular lion was quite a bit bigger than the beasts that usually visited. Bigger as in, an actual full grown male. Big. Really, really big.

He released a ground-shaking roar and Penelope steadied the stack of books that trembled on the corner of her desk. *Dammit.*

She heard him breathing heavily as he paced the length of the room. Air huffed in and out of his lungs, and she imagined his moist pink nose hovering over the ground as he sniffed the area. He was obviously hunting something—chasing his prey—she just wasn't sure what. Hell, she wasn't even sure why he bothered. The library was frequented by so many people day in and day out, lions and humans both, she didn't think he could actually find what he sought. But, whatever. Let him waste his time. She just wished he'd find it and leave already. There was a group of second graders due any moment and she hadn't had a chance to straighten the children's area.

Another roar, and this time the *other* pile wavered and actually *did* fall. *Dammit. For real this time.*

Enough was enough. She wasn't sure when Mr. Growly snuck in, but he needed to get gone. Thankfully, Penny knew just the lion to handle the job.

Her alpha, Justin Palmer.

Penny snatched up the phone and quickly dialed her alpha. There was only one ring before her call was answered, and the voice that reached her sounded panicked and harried.

"Hello?" She recognized the alpha's mate, Dana.

Since Penelope was outside the clan's den, even if no customers were in the building, she used the woman's true name rather than her title. "Hi, Dana, this is Penny down at the library. I, uh, was wondering if Justin was missing a friend from out of town."

Friend. Right.

"A friend?" The woman cleared her throat. "What kind of friend?"

"Our kind of friend." Stress on the *our*.

"Oh, thank God. Yes, yes he is, actually."

"And…" *And what the hell should I do with him?* Of course, she couldn't actually say that without sounding all disrespectful and whatnot.

"And…" She could practically hear the woman thinking. "I guess just make sure he's comfortable. At least until Justin gets there."

"Comfortable?" The woman had to be crazy. How the hell could a lion be comfortable in a freaking library? Hell, half the time Penelope wasn't comfortable. It was just that… She really enjoyed books. Well, reading books. Filing them after ankle biters got their hands on them was a different story. "You don't want to—I don't know—come get him?"

"It's not like I can actually force him to take direction, can I?" Dana snapped.

Penelope was tempted to say *yes, you really could since you're the Alpha Mate*, but refrained. She liked her hide just where it was, attached. "Okay," she swallowed past the new nervousness that attacked her, "what should I do with him then?"

The "him" in question, rounded yet another row of shelves and stopped. He swung his golden-eyed gaze to her, and it was the first time she'd actually met his stare. From the moment he'd entered the building, she'd only caught glimpses of his luxurious coat. Only seen snatches of his fluffy mane and flicking tail. Now she was trembling beneath the full weight of his gaze.

Oh, my. He was… Wow. That was all she had. Just wow.

Penelope's inner lion purred and padded forward. The cat wanted to rub and slide against the larger male. That single look made her crave him. She licked her lips, mouth suddenly dry, and she couldn't help but wonder what he'd look like on two feet rather than four. Oh, she knew he'd be tall and muscular, all male shifters were. While the females could vary in size and shape, the males—the protectors in their species—were always strong and dominant. Some more than others. This lion looked like he'd be massive in human form. Large and fierce and oh so delicious…

Yum.

No, not yum. Bad, very bad. This male wandered around like he owned the place and disrupted her entire day. Inconsiderate, that's what he was. Not yummy in any way. Except maybe in the very bad, very good way.

She was so lost. She didn't even know what he looked like, but his aggression and dominance reached out and beckoned her. Penny's cat wanted him like there was no tomorrow, and she found that her human body couldn't wait to see him once he shifted. Everything about him called to her, and she would happily pick up the phone and answer.

"You do whatever the hell he wants you to do."

Wait, where the hell did that voice come from? Oh, right. She was talking to Dana on the phone. Dana, who was telling her to do whatever he desired. Well, she had a few desires of her own. Ones that involved no clothes and lots of skin.

That's it, she was a whore. All kinds of whoredom known to whoreland.

"Considering he's looking at me like he wants to eat me for dinner, I would prefer not to do what he wants. Is there an option B?"

"No," the woman said flatly. "You don't need to know who he is, but suffice it to say, while your alpha holds your life in his hands, this male holds everyone's lives in his paws. What he wants goes. I'll let Justin know he's there."

With that, she heard the woman's phone drop into the cradle, and then a rapid dial tone filled her ear. Well, at least Dana would tell Alpha Justin where to find his wayward "friend."

Great, just great. She was left in the library, alone save a single male who looked like he had a whole different kind of eating on the brain.

The massive beast came forward, closing the distance between them, and the nearer he came, the larger he seemed. Her entire world centered on the approaching male, and fear filled her veins as she realized just how big he truly was. Dear God, if he decided he wanted to eat her for dinner, there wasn't much she'd be able to do about it. He was easily twice her size when shifted and she had no chance against him.

Her own cat reminded her she didn't want to go against him. No, she wanted to do whatever *she* wanted to do and if that included naked time, all the better. Yes, her feline was all about stripping down.

A deep rumbling purr vibrated the air and sank into her body. It slid past her flesh and deep into her bones until she felt as if it lived inside her. It touched places she didn't know existed, and she shied away from the unfamiliar sensation. She didn't know why the male affected her in such a way, but she wasn't sure she wanted to follow where the man seemed to lead. Her cat whined its objection. It ached to get closer to the lion; it wanted to bathe in his scent and bare her belly to him.

So not happening.

Penelope backed from the desk, attempting to retain the distance between their bodies, but it wasn't long before she bumped against the wall. He'd trapped her, and now there was no escape. She was gonna die. Right here, right now, she was meeting her end. What had she accomplished in life? What would people remember about her? How many people would cry at her graveside? Ugh. She was a freaking librarian. Not that there was anything wrong with being a librarian, but she had so many dreams growing up. Dreams that were about to be eaten for dinner.

Chomp. There went her pottery class.

Bite. There went her attempt at jewelry making.

Lick. There went her… Maybe licking wouldn't be so bad.

Of course, by the time she tore her attention away from licking and back to the actual lion at hand, he was there. A massive five-hundred-pound animal sat atop her steel desk, his head tilted to the side as he stared at her. His lids lowered and then rose in a sleepy, unhurried blink insinuating he didn't think of her as any threat. He wouldn't have been so slow in his perusal if he did. In reality, she wasn't a threat to anyone but unruly children who damaged her books.

"Hey, kitty. How are you?" She chuckled, hoping it sounded even remotely natural. When he merely curled his lip, revealing a single five-inch-long canine, she backtracked. "I mean, hello, how are you? Can I help you with something? I'd be happy to direct you wherever you desire to go."

Penny's lion had a lot of desires and none of them involved helping him leave. Nope, if her cat had its way, it would involve lots of skin on skin and soft surfaces. Even hard surfaces in a pinch.

The lion merely huffed, blowing a wave of moist, warm air in her direction. Not just toward her, but *into* her. Oh, boy. That... That put a whole new spin on the game.

That scent... The flavors lingered in the air and enveloped her cat in a seductive embrace. Her feline didn't just purr, it trilled and chuffed as it begged for attention. Attention and affection.

No, more than affection. It wanted so, so much more. It wanted *everything* this male had to give.

Oh, fuck her sideways. The scent of dry grassy plains and spring rain mixed with his masculine musk, as well as her cat's reaction, told her one thing. He wasn't just a gorgeous cat that smelled good. He was a gorgeous cat who belonged to her. One hundred percent totally belonged to her.

As in, this lion was her mate and she could think of nothing better than to claim him right here, right now. Was this why he'd prowled the stacks? Chasing her scent from one side of the building to the other until he finally caught sight of her?

The fanciful part of her voted "yes." It wanted to believe a male craved her so much, he could do nothing but shift and hunt.

Penny licked her lips, torn between the need to strip bare and launch herself at him and strip bare, shift, and launch herself at him. It seemed this stranger felt the same way if his fur was any indication.

He eased to the edge of the desk, claws hanging past the lip. It didn't even creak as his weight moved on honed steel. It'd been built with lions in mind, with the knowledge that cubs and adolescents alike tended to run freely and crazily when confined. He finally hopped down and his massive paws didn't make a sound as they met the carpet in front of her. Now the gorgeous male was within touching distance.

Touch, touch, touch…

Oh, dear God, she was in so much trouble. There was no measuring the amount of troublesome trouble she was in. The firm lines of his snout, the strength of his deadly jaw, the amber in his eyes, and the fullness of his mane, told her everything she needed to know. This was not a lion to be denied. He was dominant and strong, a male who made demands and expected them to be immediately satisfied.

Speaking of satisfaction…

Penelope swallowed past the growing lump in her throat, searching for her voice, and came up with nothing. Mainly because her attention was split between the glorious animal before her and her body's reaction to him. Her nipples were hard points within her bra, their heaviness aching and begging for his touch. That wasn't the only part of her that wanted him. No, her pussy grew warm and moist, silently begging to be possessed by this lion. Well, not lion-lion. More like, lion when human shaped. She wasn't into the whole lion and human boinking thing. That was just… Gross.

When the first crack of bone echoed in the silence of the building, she realized she may get her chance to get her hands on him sooner than she anticipated. Not that she truly anticipated anything. Not *realistically* anyway. She knew what she looked like and the type of man she attracted. This guy, with his air of authority and entitlement, was so out of her league. That didn't mean she couldn't look though.

Slowly, carefully, with unerring precision, he was revealed.

Massive paws receded to reveal equally large hands, thick forearms and biceps came next, and his chest seemed just as wide in his human shape as he'd been when he wore fur. He was a study in carved muscle and bone, and she didn't hesitate to drink her fill with her gaze. He was strength personified, and she wanted to climb him like a motherfucking tree.

During her perusal, she kinda sorta skipped over the "junk" area. She was all for staring, but it was a little rude to ogle a man after a shift. Shifters had standards of conduct.

She did allow herself to focus on his face, seeing remnants of the man's beast in his features. The jaw, his nose, and the fierceness in his eyes. Eyes that seemed to delve into her—their startling amber hue still in place, telling her his beast was still very, very close to the surface. He changed position ever so slightly, brushing a tendril of long midnight hair over his broad shoulders, drawing her back to his nude body. *No, bad, Penelope, bad.*

A low, masculine chuckle shook his frame and had her refocusing on his face again. On the wide spread of his lips and the seductive smile that curved his mouth.

He really shouldn't smile. Ever. Because the moment that expression settled into place, her panties were wet with arousal. Did he leave hundreds of women with wet panties in his wake? Probably. And he didn't seem repentant in anyway.

"That's because I'm not," his words vibrated the air and crawled through her.

"What?"

"I don't care that I leave a trail of wet panties behind me. Because they're *behind* me. The only panties I care about are yours." He stepped closer, his scorching heat branding her skin. "Tell me, sweetheart, are yours?"

He was asking her a question? He wanted her to think? Penny tried really hard—she totally did—but words failed her. She couldn't grasp anything when her mind and body were enraptured by his delicious scent and overwhelming presence. And his skin, so much skin. She wanted to lick him from head to toe, taste every inch, and see if the small spot at the base of his throat tasted the same as that deeply carved line on his hip.

The stranger's wicked grin turned smoldering, and she whimpered at the sensual promises that lingered in his features. Then his nostrils flared, his chest expanding as he drew in a breath, and he released it with a deep purr.

"Yes, yes they are wet."

Suddenly she was in his arms, his grip holding her flush against him, and his warmth really did brand her. She was surrounded by him, enveloped by him, and she never wanted to be anywhere else.

He buried his fingers in her hair, forcing her to tilt her head back, and she found herself lost in his gaze. Penny trembled beneath his stare and it was as if her lungs forgot how to breathe, her heart forgot how to send blood rushing through her veins, and all she could do was meet his intense stare and wait for his next move. It wasn't long in coming. His lips met hers in a searing kiss, one that overpowered her and stole any objection that may have lingered on her lips.

Objection? Ha! Not likely.

He controlled their passionate meeting, his tongue venturing into her mouth, licking and tasting her. She fought to do the same, explore his heated flavors, but he was too much. He overpowered her with ease, taking what he desired and she was unable—unwilling—to object. Not when his massive hands cupped her ass and lifted her against him, not when he yanked her skirt to her waist and then encouraged her to wrap her legs around his hips, or when his shaft came in contact with the fabric-covered juncture of her thighs. It was too much and not enough, his touch wandering over her, consuming her more and more with each passing second.

Growls and snarls followed each movement, as if staking his claim with his body wasn't enough. He seemed to want to fill the air with trembling warnings.

And wasn't that fucking hot?

When his lips left her mouth long enough to trail kisses along her throat, she took a moment to drag in much needed air. He scraped the column of her neck with his deadly fangs, scratching her skin and sending a bolt of the delicious pain down her spine. Then he… nearly had her coming due to his voice alone.

"Mine." He growled against her shoulder. "*Mine*."

It seemed as if he was searching for confirmation, and she was quick to give it. She was his, just as he was hers. "*Mine*. You're mine."

He ripped and tore at the fabric that covered her skin, and she cursed the fact she wore clothes to work. Obviously she had to wear *something* because of the kiddies, but if she'd come naked, this whole process would have gone a lot quicker. She wanted skin on skin, his cock inside her and his teeth in her shoulder. ASAP.

Her skirt was gone in a moment, her top suffering the same fate, and her bra and panties were no barrier to his razor-sharp nails. Then it truly was flesh against flesh, his shaft rubbing against her moistness, and the blunted head of his length was poised at her entrance.

Ideally, knowing his name before taking this momentous step would be a big deal, but… *Mates.* There was no denying the truth, and when it came to shifters, it tended to be mate first, talk second. Or rather seventy-fifth since all the moments before were spent mating. So, yeah, she was all with getting down and dirty despite the lack of names and their current location. She would disinfect everything later. Much, much later.

"Please, please, please…" she didn't care that she was begging and pleading with this guy. There was no pride when it came to being with her other half.

He didn't say much, but what he did say, had her hovering on the edge of release with that single syllable. "Mine."

"Yes," she hissed. All kinds of yes.

Except somebody had to be the one and only asshole in the world and interrupt them. "No!"

Penelope clutched her mate's shoulders, clinging to him not because she was desperate for his body, but for protection. She whimpered, uneasy at the intrusion, and her emotions wavered between desperate for her mate and fear that someone was denying their mating.

He released her, and in a sudden whirl, had her pinned behind him as he faced off against their intruder. His previous sounds had nothing on the ground-shaking roar that vibrated the entire building. The floor rolled and trembled with the sound, and she steadied herself by placing her hands on his back. He shuddered with her touch and gently leaned toward her. He seemed to take comfort in the connection, but his threatening sounds did not cease.

"Alpha, I mean no disrespect." The intruder's tone was familiar and Penelope swallowed the groan that leapt to her lips. Her den's alpha. *Of course*, Justin would find them together. She'd called his house, hadn't she? She should have held off on the panic attack a little longer.

She waited for the man to continue. There was a "but" in there somewhere. And… It wasn't long in coming. "But I don't wish for you to make a mistake that would ruin the rest of your life."

Well, she knew Alpha Palmer disliked her, but she didn't realize he felt she would ruin someone's life by claiming her mate. So nice to be loved by her own pride.

The male blocking her view renewed his threatening growls, and she stroked his back, urging him to calm. Two alphas going at each other's throat in the middle of the library was so not a good thing. Blood didn't exactly wash out of books easily and her budget wasn't big enough to replace the ones these two would ruin.

"Mine." Penny wondered if her mate knew any other word.

"I understand how you're feeling, but it isn't real." Alpha Palmer's voice was low and soothing. At least she assumed that was the tone he was going for. It was kinda hard for a male who lived his life giving orders and growling at the world to actually sound soothing. “This isn’t real. She isn’t your mate. She’d ruin—”

“Another word and I will rip out your throat.” Apparently her mate could string words together. Very threatening words, at that.

“You’re under a spell, Alpha. A witch was detained just outside of town. She admitted to casting a spell on you.” Justin pleaded with her mate. “We don’t know what she’s done, but look at your actions.” Alpha Palmer gestured toward Penelope. “Do you imagine a woman like her as your mate? Truly, Alpha, think before you do something you’ll regret.”

She swallowed hard, battling the sob that formed in her chest and threatened to burst from her mouth. Regret? Rest of his life? He was her *mate*. How could anyone ever regret claiming their mate? But she felt her mate’s resolve wavering. It was in the way his shoulders relaxed slightly, the disappearance of the fur that coated his arms, and the receding of his claws until his hands were human once again. He was listening to Alpha Palmer. He was listening to the man before them rather than following his beast’s instincts.

Could it be true? Was there a spell cast on her mate? Was he even really her mate at all?

Why was she even asking the question? Of course he was her mate. If a spell was cast on *him*, it wouldn't affect her. And she was very, very affected by him.

"Alpha Palmer…" She peeked around her mate's body. "I don't think—"

"You're right, don't think," he snapped.

Penny flinched beneath the man's anger and hid behind her mate once again. A mate who did not seem intent on destroying Justin for acting aggressively toward her. So, he believed Alpha Palmer. It shouldn't hurt, not when they didn't even know each other's names, and yet… It did. It more than hurt, it crushed her heart. Maybe it was a spell that brought him to her library doors, but it wasn't a spell that had her lioness craving the man before her. It wasn't a spell that had her more than willing to mate the male in the middle of the building for one and all to see. Didn't her mate recognize that? Or her alpha?

No, he didn't. Because he next stepped forward, putting space between them, and spoke to Alpha Palmer. "A witch?"

She leaned her head against the wall at her back and closed her eyes, refusing to look at her could-have-been mate any longer. Instead, she simply listened to their conversation.

"Yes, our local caster has her magically tied to a plot of land at the edge of town. If you like, we can get you some clothes and address the situation."

"I… see." After her mate's two words, quiet returned.

Yes, silence enveloped them, but the tension remained high and cloying. It seemed oppressive and weighed against her body until she could no longer stand beneath its power.

She scented the room, cataloging each flavor from the men. There was pure, true conviction in her alpha's aromas and her mate's emotions were slowly easing toward acceptance and belief. A lion couldn't lie and Justin was so sure he was right…

The two men seem to be in a standoff of sorts, but enough was enough. Penny had endured a near mating, had her childhood dreams almost in her grasp, only to have them ripped from her by one of her own pride. Nothing new to her. Now, she was simply tired. She wanted to gather what was left of her clothes and make an elegant-ish retreat.

"Excuse me," she used the tone that often worked on the younger patrons of the library. "I believe it is time you both departed. I would like to straighten the library, and then I'll be going home."

She left no room for argument, and instead of waiting for their agreement, she merely stepped from behind her mate and went to her desk. She ignored the male's growl, knowing he had no right to take issue with her exposing herself to Justin, and instead withdrew the extra set of clothing she kept in the bottom drawer. It was there in case there was an emergency shifting situation but also because the children who came in occasionally got a little too rowdy with their markers.

She spared neither male a glance as she tugged on the comfortable pants and equally soft top. She didn't have a set of bra and panties on hand, but she didn't plan on rocking the clothing for very long. They could leave, she could clean, and then her day would end with a nice long, hot bath and a good cry.

At this point, she figured she'd earned a good sob session. Because in a span of fifteen minutes, she'd found and lost her mate.

The moment she was covered, she turned to face the men. She first focused on her mate, giving him a grim and yet rueful smile. "It was nice meeting you." He opened his mouth to reply, but she refused to listen to whatever he had to say. Instead, she stared at her alpha. "Alpha Palmer, thank you for saving him from what you believe would have been a mistake."

"It would—"

"As I said, thank you." She didn't leave any room for him to speak further. And when he glared at her, she refused to be intimidated. He was a strong lion—there was no doubt about that—but everyone knew she was quite a bit stronger. As she was growing up, it had been yet another line in the list of reasons half the town disliked her. She didn't look like the typical lioness, she didn't cower like a typical lioness, but she also didn't fight for dominance and status like a typical lioness. Add in the fact that her family tree was "colorful" and included vamps, witches, and humans…

"Penelope—"

"I'll see you at the next gathering." She spun on her heel, and moved toward the stacks, unwilling to hear another word from *him*. She'd lose herself in the books and pray she could lose her emotional pain just as easily. When her mate's deep voice reached out and stroked her, she knew she'd never forget those few moments when she held happiness in her arms. Nor would she forget who'd destroyed her dreams.

With luck, and more control than she ever thought she possessed, she managed to keep her tears at bay. It wasn't until she was alone with her own thoughts, and her own heartache, that the first trailed down her cheek to stain the book in her lap.

* * *

It was amazing what a person could have delivered nowadays. Because Penelope was now the proud owner of buttercream iced cupcakes, more ice cream than she could consume in one sitting, and several bottles of wine to top it off.

Now, staring at it all on her kitchen counter, she couldn't decide what to jump into first. She knew she could drown her sorrows in each option, but when it came down to it, what would gorging herself accomplish?

Nothing. But maybe she could convince herself for a moment that she hadn't had happiness within reach. And then torn away just as quickly.

Well, if she wanted to blunt her feelings, she'd begin with the wine. She grabbed the bottle opener from its home and went to work on the first bottle she snagged. She loved them all, so she didn't really care where she started or ended.

She was working on the first cork when the rapid pounding of a fist on her front door interrupted. It wasn't heavy and strong like a male's, and she banished the small hint of joy that'd blossomed in her chest. It was a witch's spell, remember? It wasn't like he was going to come find her. It wasn't like he felt the same as her. It wasn't like—

Another round of banging on the metal panel, and it was joined by a familiar voice. "Dammit,

Penny, open this door!" Another speedy series of thumps. "I mean it!"

With a sigh, she placed the bottle and opener on the counter and padded toward the front door. She loved having a best friend… When said best friend wasn't trying to interrupt her pity party. She undid the locks, turned the knob, and tugged the panel open. "Jennifer."

Sympathy filled the other woman's gaze and Penelope tore her attention from her friend, unwilling to suffer under the expression. She didn't want anyone to feel badly for her. She wanted to be left alone. It was bad enough that half the pride laughed at her on a regular basis while the other half sneered, but now with recent events… There would be no hiding from their torment. She knew it was only a matter of time before Alpha Palmer "encouraged" her to find a new pride. With today's events, she imagined the order would come any time now.

"Oh God, Penelope." Penelope's own heartache was mirrored on her best friend's features and the dam broke.

"Jennifer…" The first cry escaped, and then it was downhill from there.

Hugs were shared, tears were wiped, noses were very unsexily blown, and more than enough wine was consumed. By the time they finished their second bottle, Penelope managed to release the whole sordid, seriously not long enough, tale. From the first grumble, to the first purr, and on to the first taste of his skin, she revealed all. There were no secrets from the woman who'd stood by her side year after year despite the teasing and poor treatment by the rest of their pride.

"So, that's it." Penelope drained the last few drops from her glass.

"That's it?" Jennifer slammed her delicate glass on the coffee table and winced, waiting for it to shatter. Amazingly, it did not. "*Justin*," her best friend sneered, "strides in, interrupts, claims some witch is behind it all, and *that's it*?"

Justin… For a moment, Penelope forgot that Justin was Jennifer's brother which was why the woman could even *talk* about the man with such a disrespectful tone. But just for a moment.

"Yup." She reached for another bottle. Knowing they were likely to drain them all, they had yanked the cork on each one before they began. "Pretty much."

"You're joking."

"Nope."

"But… But…" Jennifer sputtered. "He's wrong."

"I doubt it." Fuck it. She was probably on the way out anyway. She could be disrespectful too. Penelope deepened her voice to imitate Alpha Palmer. "My decisions are final and unbreakable. You do not deny me, you do not disobey me. My word is law."

"But it's not." Jennifer shook her head. "The spell didn't pick Marcus. It doesn't work that way."

Marcus… Marcus was a nice name… It was sexy and sinful and it tasted delicious. "Marcus…" Penelope turned her head until she could stare at her friend. "Is that his name? Marcus…"

"You didn't even know his name? You don't know who he is?"

"Should I? We kind of skipped that part. He was a lion, then he was human, then he had his tongue in my throat. We jumped over everything else." She sighed happily. "Did I mention how sexy he was? And the whole mating thing?"

The mating thing. Or rather, the not mating thing. The not mating thing and the embarrassment that came from the entire process being stopped by Alpha Palmer.

"...a mistake that would ruin the rest of your life."

"Yes, you mentioned that," her friend drawled. "I'll fill you in on your mate then."

Penelope shook her head and fought the dizziness that came with the action. "No, he's not my mate. We just discussed this, didn't we?"

"Humor me." Jennifer reached for her previously discarded glass and refilled it before sitting back once again. "His name is Marcus Tolson."

"That name sounds familiar."

The woman grinned at her and tried to hide the smile behind the glass but failed miserably.

"Yes, I imagine it would. Especially considering he's the North American Alpha."

Oh. Right. Nice. *Super nice.*

Penelope groaned and flopped sideways, burying her face in a pillow. "Now I know he's not my mate. I'm so not North American Alpha Mate material." She was fluffy, average mate material. She moaned again. "I assaulted the North American Alpha."

"No," her friend began, "you tried to claim your mate."

"Did you sorta miss the part where he was under the spell of a witch?" Her words were muffled but she had no doubt Jennifer heard her. "I was pretty sure that part was covered."

"And I *said* the spell didn't work that way."

Now, admittedly, Penelope's brain was quite muddled by the mass consumption of wine—it took a lot to get a lion drunk—but the lioness' words tickled her brain. She fought to push herself up but did nothing more than flop around like a fish on sand. Giving up, she finally just settled in place and decided to have this conversation from her sprawled position.

"And how, my very best friend in the whole wide world, do you know how the spell works?" A very telling, very, very damning silence was Jennifer's answer. "What, my very best friend in the whole wide world, did you do?"

More silence, but Penelope decided to wait Jennifer out. She didn't care if it took five seconds or five hours, her best friend had a lot to answer for. Because now, new thoughts churned through her alcohol-muddled mind. Ones that said maybe Marcus truly *was* her mate. That it was Alpha Palmer who was wrong. That it was really okay for Penelope to climb Marcus like a tree.

"Well… You see… Hypothetically I may, or may not have, contracted the services of a certain witch who happens to hypothetically… Did I mention hypothetically? Hypothetically be a relative of yours. Which is why the possible spell worked so well for you and had Marcus chasing your scent across the country."

Penelope groaned and squeezed her eyes shut. "And what, exactly and non-hypothetically, did you ask her to do?"

"I may or may not have—"

"Dammit," Penelope snarled. "This is my life, Jennifer." She forced her head up and glared at the other lioness. "What the fuck did you do?" In response to her aggressive tone, Jennifer's eyes filled with tears, a single drop of moisture making its way down her cheek. That had her burying her face once again. "You're such a crier when you're drunk. It takes the fun out of yelling at you." She sighed. "Tell me already."

"I just wanted you to be happy. You've been miserable for so long. You've dealt with so much. Your parents… This pride…" Jennifer's cool small hands grasped Penelope's and squeezed gently. "You deserve to be happy, Penny."

Penelope remained silent, knowing if she tried to make a sound, the pain of her past and the agony of her present would overwhelm her. Yes, most of her life had been shit. She was a mutt and then there was the fact that her parents never supported her. Oh, they put a roof over her head and made sure they gave her the necessities, but emotionally…

They were disgraced by her. They could have dealt with her curvy body. Her best friend—the old alpha's daughter—was a little rounded, after all. But combined with her behavior… It was too much for them. She didn't act like a "real" lion. She didn't crave the hunt or embrace the natural dominance that lived inside her. She had too much non-shifter DNA in her blood that overrode her cat.

Her failure as a lioness upset her father, which meant her mother was frustrated with her for disappointing her mate even though it was her mother's genetics that made Penelope the way she was. Their continued tension and strife put them in a vulnerable position within the pride until Penelope was shunted aside to maintain family harmony. Well, harmony for them. Because their private rejection wasn't quite so private and it influenced how others treated her. Even after her parents passed, she was treated with disrespect.

Did she deserve to be happy when she caused so much pain to others? She didn't even think she deserved to ask that question.

"I'm fine. I've been fine for a long time. I have a good life, I have a job I love, and—"

"And you're alone."

"But I'm happy."

Jennifer shook her head. "No, you're really not. You can't lie to me."

"Jen… just say it."

"I found the most powerful woman on your witch side of the family tree, and when I told her everything about you, she agreed with me. She came to town and worked her magic mojo." A sudden excitement filled the air and her best friend squirmed in her seat. "And for *free*."

"Well, I'm glad it didn't cost you anything since it didn't work because of the whole 'getting caught' thing."

"Weren't you listening? It *did* work. It was only meant to bring your mate here. Not Larry, not Joe Bob from two counties over, not Pierre from across the pond." Jennifer shrugged. "Just your mate."

Penelope let those words sink into her, let them crawl through her blood and along her veins, let them creep into her bones, and felt them flick something deep inside her. It stroked the certainty in her heart that he was her mate. The belief that Marcus was her mate despite what they'd been told. Was he really?

Her cat answered for her with a resounding roar. It knew the truth, and it clawed aside her human's worries and concerns. Her hint of hesitation, her sliver of doubt, gave the beast a chance to rush forward. It assured her that Marcus belonged to them, he was theirs and no other's, and it was time they got their shit together and went and got him.

"He's mine."

"Yes."

The cat pushed forward, shoving the human parts of her to the background as it stole control of her two-footed form. Its rush burned away the alcohol in her veins, clearing her mind of the liquid's cloud. She rolled to her feet, body prepped and primed and aching for her mate. It wasn't a question. "Marcus Tolson, North American Alpha, is *mine*. And it's time he accepted it."

Her hands ached, and she allowed even more of the feline to push forward, her nails transforming to sharp claws. Her gums throbbed and then her fangs descended pricking her lower lip. The lioness' strength that she always brushed aside was in full force as she embraced her dominant urges.

"Whoa." Jennifer's gaze moved over her from head to toe. "This whole angry look is kinda sexy. If I swung your way, I'd be all over you."

Shaking her head, Penelope plucked the half-full glass from her best friend's grip and snagged the remaining bottle of wine as well. "Come on, let's get you sobered up a little, and then you can tell me where to find Marcus. Your brother may have interfered once, but I'll be damned if it happens again."

Jennifer pushed to her feet, body swaying slightly, and she studied Penelope carefully. "I know you've always been strong and just disregarded that part of you, but since Marcus is your mate, that means you're actually a really, *really* strong lion. Stronger than any of us." Jennifer hiccupped. "Like, I bet if you snarled a little, you could even get Justin to roll over and bare his belly." Her best friend jumped in place and released an excited squeal. "Ooh, say you'll do it, say you'll do it!"

The idea had merit, but Penelope had something to accomplish first. Mainly, making Marcus Tolson hers and begging him to do the same in return. With any luck, it wouldn't require any bloodshed. Or at least, not a lot.

"We'll discuss it on the way. Where can we find them all?" Because she had no doubt Marcus and Justin didn't go alone to question the witch. Or rather, her relative.

Her best friend paused in her excited bouncing. "Oh. They're at your house."

Penelope's house. Or rather the place she'd lived until she was forced out. True, it still remained in her name, but she hadn't been there in more years than she could count. It held so many memories... None she wanted to keep.

Sensing her disquiet, Jennifer grasped Penelope's hand and twined their fingers. "You can do it, Pen. It's just a house."

Sure, it was just the house. Penelope didn't tell Jennifer it wasn't just the house. It was hell. A hell that currently held her ticket to heaven.

"Besides," Jennifer continued, "if we don't get there before Justin introduces her to Marcus, there's no telling what will happen. Angry alphas aren't necessarily understanding alphas and Marcus has plenty to be angry about if he believes my brother. Justin has already poisoned his mind against you and the witch.

What's going to happen to her if a furious Marcus gets to her first?"

She'll be torn to shreds.

"Dammit," she snarled. "Let's go."

CHAPTER TWO

Marcus would rip off the head of the next lion who spoke to him. Hell, the next person, lion or human, who spoke to him would die. His inner cat was in full agreement. The animal was agitated and anxious to tear into everyone in the room. Each time the air conditioner kicked on, each time someone came near, he was assaulted with different scents. Males and females, musk and perfume, sweat and earth… They surrounded him in the cloying room.

His skin itched, his fur rippling through his flesh only to disappear once again. Each wave he banished proved just how strong his lion was becoming as the seconds passed. It would slide fur free of his pores, and just as quickly Marcus would regain control and the light dusting of gold would vanish. He was the North American Alpha, the strongest lion on the continent. He didn't have the luxury of losing control. When his animal snatched the human's power, there was no telling what would be left in his wake. The way he felt that moment, he knew it would be a trail of blood and gore.

Mainly because everyone in the vicinity was attempting to keep him from one single, luscious female.

Penelope Little. She was tiny compared to him, short and compact with generous curves that had cradled him so sweetly. She was a handful and then some, built for him from head to toe. It was as if God himself crept into Marcus' brain and discovered what he viewed as the ideal woman.

Yes, the average lioness was lithe and lean, but that wasn't what turned on Marcus. He liked the softness of a curved female, the ways she molded to his hard body, and the way her form contrasted so heavily against his. He had enough hardness in his day-to-day life. Sometimes a male just needed a daily dose of sweetness to make it from one day to the next.

With him that was doubly important. He battled his near indestructible lion on a daily basis, fought it to prove his dominance over every being he came across. But with her in his arms that need and unshakable desire was blunted.

For the first time in his life, he could breathe and relax without the fear of harming someone. Hell, he hadn't killed Justin Palmer, had he? The pre-Penelope Marcus would have ripped the head off the male for interrupting him before returning to the woman he'd held so close.

Instead, he'd been the ultimate asshole and removed his touch. Yes, he'd hidden her from Palmer's gaze, but the second a sliver of doubt assaulted him, he left her to survive on her own.

Since when do I listen to anyone else? I'm the North American motherfucking Alpha.

Voices layered over voices, males and females whirling together until he couldn't discern one from the next. No, it wasn't them that kept his mind from settling, it was his animal and his body screaming for Penelope that kept him from focusing. Even now, hours later, he was rock hard and anxious to slide into her warmth and wetness, and eventually her heart.

Oh, he knew and understood what everyone told him; a witch had cast a spell on him, making him feel as if Penelope belonged to him. But… He couldn't shake the feeling they were wrong. It wasn't just his behavior in the library. It was so much more.

It was that "more" that fueled his unwavering desire to travel across country. His unending drive to head south. His refusal to go anywhere but the small town of Ryland…

Unable to stand another moment in anyone's presence, he pushed to his feet. The fluid move drew everyone's attention and silence immediately fell over the room. The house, the pride den, was large. Especially considering the size of the small group in this tiny southern town, but it wasn't big enough for him. He could still smell Penelope on his skin, refusing a shower after he'd arrived at the den, but the flavors in the room were overpowering her natural aromas. His beast needed to smell her in her purest form. In order to do that, he needed to be away… Away from here… Away from everyone.

"Alpha?" Palmer was the first to risk speaking to him.

Surprising. It seemed the local alpha had no sense of self-preservation. If he had, he wouldn't have said a word directly to Marcus. Even Marcus' own guard detail had remained silent from the moment they'd left the library. After so many years, the men were sensitive to his moods.

"Can I get you something?" The local alpha tried again.

Marcus carefully, slowly, turned his golden gaze to the large male. Large, but not larger than Marcus. He wasn't meaner or deadlier than him either. He would really, really like to release some of that deadliness right about now.

Without a word, Marcus spun on his heel and moved to the front door. His steps were silent over the hardwood, even his boots not daring to make a noise on the solid surface.

At the moment, he was pure predator, pure animal, pure unadulterated rage. There was a scramble behind him, shuffles of the room's occupants struggling to their feet. The immediate sound of a low grunt from someone told him his guards had done their jobs.

They'd obviously knocked back a lion and kept them from chasing after Marcus. No one would follow him, no one would dare. Not when the males in his entourage explained that Marcus would destroy the next person who spoke in his presence. His lion would allow for nothing less. Whether he was battling a witch's spell or the natural desire for his true mate, he couldn't be trusted at the moment.

He burst from the house, shoving the front door wide, and the moment he was free he breathed deeply. He drew in the clean scents of the country air, sucking it into his body, and he sighed when his beast relaxed the tiniest bit. Some of the tension thrumming in his veins vanished with the nature surrounding him. This was where his lion belonged, where all the lions belonged. Nature, trees, grasses, live prey, and open plains to run.

Did his mate enjoy these acres as much as Marcus' own animal? He didn't doubt it. She wouldn't be a true match for him if she didn't and he hoped she wouldn't mind leaving it all behind.

They'd address the problem *if* she was a match. Marcus shook his head, still unable to accept the alpha's assertions that a witch held so much power over him.

He yanked his shirt from his body, letting it drop to the ground. There, he could breathe again. Breathe in her scent that lingered on his skin. She'd touched and stroked him, whimpering and whining as her tongue slid over his skin. Growling when her teeth nipped his flesh. He shuddered, the memory of that small sting shooting through his blood.

The low squeak and then heavy thump of boots on the front porch reached him and it was immediately followed by the familiar scent of his best friend and captain of his guard. The male could have his own pride, or even act as Marcus' Beta, but the lion constantly refused.

"I get enough tail just following you around. Why the fuck do I gotta take on some title when I already get everything I need, and all I gotta do is save your ass once in a while?"

With each new breath, Penelope's aroma was overrun by Lincoln's until Marcus was ready to cut the male to shreds. His body called for Penelope, thickness rock hard and primed to fill her, and his friend's presence was destroying his mate's lingering flavors. Dammit, he'd come outside to be alone, to revel in what was left of his mate on his body.

He spun in place, a snarl on his lips, and bared his fangs at Lincoln. Instead of cowering, or even flinching beneath Marcus' fury, the male simply leaned against a porch support post and crossed his ankles.

"Got that out of the way, now?" Lincoln drawled.

Marcus merely narrowed his eyes and glared at his best friend. "What do you want?"

The other man shrugged. "Just want to know what we're going to do next."

He closed his eyes, coaxing his lion away from the front of his mind so he could think for a moment. Think without the cloud of driving need and desperation for one particular curvy female. He was the North American Alpha for a reason, and it wasn't merely because he could kick everyone else's ass. He was also analytical, intelligent, and operated with a calm that was out of reach for the average lion. Not that his current behavior was an example of that ability.

"I don't trust Palmer." Marcus wasn't sure why, wasn't sure what caused him to form that opinion. It wasn't as if the local alpha had done anything specific to mislead him. Or had he?

The low growl that emanated from within the house told him the man heard Marcus' words. He mentally shrugged. He hoped he wouldn't have to kick the idiot lion's ass, but if he did, he did. He wasn't insulting the man—not much anyway—but he was a damn good judge of character and behavior. There was something about this Justin Palmer… Something about the male and Penelope.

"…a mistake that would ruin the rest of your life."

Now, why would an alpha say that about one of his own lions? If anything, Marcus mating one of Justin's pride would benefit every cat in the town. And yet it would somehow ruin Marcus' life?

He wasn't buying it. Now that some of his desire for Penelope was easing back and he could think clearly, he realized he needed to have a claw-to-claw conversation with the male.

Marcus took a deep, calming breath, allowing his lion to savor one last taste of Penelope's scent. He released it with a long sigh and then focused his mind on the problem in front of him. Particularly the local alpha's beliefs and how he'd come to those conclusions.

"I want to talk to Palmer and the witch. Together. Now."

Lincoln pushed away from the post and rose to his full height. "All right then."

Marcus remained in place, ignoring the snarls and hisses that came from within the home. His men would do their job quickly and efficiently. He wouldn't have long to wait, and within thirty seconds he had one almost trembling alpha standing before him. Oh, he had to respect the male for his attempt at remaining strong and tall beneath the weight of Marcus' anger, but it didn't change the fact that Marcus would get his way.

He reached for Palmer and wrapped his hand around the back of the male's neck, yanking him forward until he walked at Marcus' side toward the waiting vehicle. "You're going to give Lincoln, here, directions to where we can find the witch. And then we're all going to have a chat."

"A-a-alpha… do you think—"

"Really not a good idea to ask questions at this point," Lincoln inserted smoothly, which saved Marcus from having to sink his claws into the male's neck.

Hell, Marcus might not have even stopped there. Especially once the lion realized Palmer's blood would drive away what remained of Penelope's flavors on his skin and *that* was unforgivable as far as the cat was concerned.

It took moments for them to climb into the nearest SUV, the rest of Marcus' group piling into others, and then they were on their way. The local alpha's voice trembled as he gave directions, and Marcus imagined Palmer was finally understanding his position—one of a lion suffering beneath the North American Alpha's displeasure.

"Go through the gates at the end of the road," Palmer swallowed hard, the action audible in the quiet confines of the SUV. "And then it's another five hundred yards down that dirt road." The local alpha shot Marcus a brief glance. "She's confined to the land at the moment. Entering her domain puts you at risk, Alpha."

"I understand." Marcus held on to his rage by a thread. The closer they got to this mysterious witch, the more certain he became that Justin Palmer was wrong, and Penelope Little was very, very right. For him.

They rounded the last bend, emerging from the untamed trees that filled their vision, and the home before him nearly stole his breath. With its wide wraparound porch and tall pillars, it looked as if it had been plucked out of history, a southern plantation house that begged to be filled by a family.

Damn, if that thought wasn't proof enough that he'd found his mate, he wasn't sure what else could drive the thought home. Marcus Tolson? A family? He hadn't ever craved one, but with Penelope on the brain…

The moment the vehicle rolled to a stop, Marcus was free of the SUV and striding toward the woman on the porch who seemed to be waiting for their arrival. He cataloged her appearance in a brief sweep, noting the features were similar to the woman he thought of as his mate.

"Alpha!" Palmer shouted for him, but that yell was quickly followed by an echoing snarled and then a grunt.

Lincoln was having too much fun taking out his frustration on the local alpha.

Marcus bounded up the steps, only slowing when he stood mere feet from the woman. He sensed her magic, the power within her seeming to glow and emanate from her skin.

"Mistress," he tilted his head in acknowledgment, but not submission. He recognized her abilities but refused to be cowed or frightened by them.

"Georgie will do." She gave him a rueful smile. "So, what did the idiot tell you?"

"That you're a witch. The question is what kind."

That smile turned from rueful to teasing. "Didn't your mama ever tell you that asking a woman what kind of witch she is, is akin to asking a woman her age?" She winked at him.

"Okay," he crossed his arms over his chest. "If you won't tell me that, tell me if there's a reason why I shouldn't kill you right now. Interfering with a lion's mating, especially an alpha's, is a death offense."

"I didn't realize helping you find your mate was interfering," she mused. "I could take her away from you." She snapped her fingers. "Like that."

Marcus growled. "So you're saying she's mine?"

"I'm saying—"

She was cut off by the loud, obnoxious honk of an approaching vehicle, the small car bursting into the clearing surrounding the house in a storm of dust and flying rocks. The very second the vehicle stopped, its driver was free and racing over the ground. He had an instant vision of her luscious body, an image of a stripping and then nude Penelope seared in his brain. At least until she was suddenly replaced by a roaring, running lioness.

Her anger, her fury, struck him a split second before her furious body tackled him to the ground. He should be furious, raging and destroying the woman who'd broken past his guards and pounced with such ease. She had dominance over him, her teeth a hair's breadth from his vulnerable throat and her saliva dripped onto his skin.

Yes, he should shift his hands into deadly claws and shove her from his body before taking her to the porch's worn flooring. And yet, his only thought was that she smelled so damned good. Her sweetness, her seductive flavors, beckoned his animal forward. But not to do battle. No, to mate and claim her before anyone could interrupt them once again.

Other sounds filled the clearing, more of the lions going after each other, words being slung across the space, but a feminine shout rose above the rest.

"Don't you fucking hurt her!" It was an order, plain and simple, followed by a muffled grumble. "Stop touching me, dammit. Let me go. I will rip your balls off through your throat, don't see if I won't."

If Marcus wasn't close to losing his life to his mate, he'd find the spunky female fighting with his guards funny.

"I mean it! I will hunt you like the poor excuse for a feline that you are," the woman yelled again, and those words were followed by a few choice threats from Lincoln.

That had Penelope, seductive and furious Penelope, tightening her hold on his flesh. Dammit, he was rock fucking hard, and rather than focusing on the fact he was moments from being killed, all he could think about was slipping into her over and over. He wanted her now just as much as he had that morning. Maybe more so.

Marcus' gaze was intent on her, her pale eyes boring into him as if she could see into his soul, and he fought to do the same. He wanted to know everything about her, everything that made her tick, everything that made her laugh and cry.

The strange female and Lincoln continued to argue, and he saw the indecision and worry that lingered in Penelope's eyes. While she'd been all over him mere hours ago with sex on the brain, she had a completely different purpose now. She'd come after him, true, but he didn't imagine it was because of him, but probably because of his proximity to the witch. Further, the increase in her anxiety and aggression had to do with Lincoln and the other woman.

"Lincoln, cut out that shit and let her go." His friend grunted, and he imagined the woman had taken a shot at him when his friend followed Marcus' orders.

That had him smiling even if he was so close to death. His human half was slightly concerned by that fact while his lion half was aroused by his mate's strength and determination.

"Jennifer!" That was Palmer, and the woman's name was familiar to him. Justin Palmer had a twin sister. Jennifer. The female was obviously protective of Penelope which made her one of Marcus' new favorite people.

"Oh, fuck off, asshole."

"I am your—"

"Brother. You're my brother. And if you so much as touch a hair on my head, Dad will so come back and kick your ass, so shut the fuck up before Penelope kills someone."

That had Palmer snorting, and Marcus decided the male wouldn't live past the day. *Anyone* underestimating his mate and belittling her abilities was asking for trouble.

The soft careful steps of someone approaching, a light someone, signaled they'd soon have a visitor.

Georgie entered his line of sight, and her wide smile was nearly blinding. "Penelope, dear, perhaps you should let your pretty mate go. I don't think there's a reason to kill him, not when he has such a pretty, pretty package."

Marcus wasn't sure if the witch spoke of his physical appearance or the fact he was full and large in his jeans. Either way, his lion objected to the description. His body was only up for comment by his mate. The fact that any other female dare speak of him in that way enraged the beast. It didn't want to hear compliments from anyone but Penelope. When the lioness began audibly growling and quickly released him to snap at the witch, he knew she felt the same.

"There, that's better." He heard the contented smile in her voice, even if he could no longer see her, his vision now consumed by the gold of Penelope's fur. "Now, I believe someone has questions for me."

Another body blurred in his periphery and Jennifer Palmer joined the conversation. "Us. Questions for *us*. Georgie didn't do it alone."

"And what," Georgie drawled, "could a lion possibly do when it came to casting spells?"

Jennifer tried to answer. "I—"

But Marcus had only one question. "Is Penelope truly my mate?"

Silence was his answer, the lack of sound was oppressive as seconds ticked past, but finally the witch replied. "I only called Penelope's mate. I didn't *make* her your mate, I simply encouraged the male who belonged to her to find her."

Somehow he grew harder, filling even more. "Short answer is yes, then."

"Yes," Georgie confirmed.

The "yes" was all he needed, all that was necessary for him to let the lion finally have free rein with his body. He wanted her, and he accepted and embraced the desires pounding through. He had her and he wasn't about to let her go. Not until he claimed her every way he possibly could. Twice. Okay, maybe five times.

And that was only the first day. He couldn't wait for the rest of their lives.

Penelope must have scented his arousal because she shuddered, a small tremble shaking her body, and then she released a deep seductive purr.

It was as if they were back in the library, both of their bodies working overtime, desire and craving wrapping them in a desperate blanket of arousal.

"Good." He didn't bother addressing anyone but the single male who could get shit done and fast. "Lincoln, get everyone the fuck out of here. Now. And if someone so much as gets within one thousand feet of this house before I make Penelope mine, they'll be dead. Make sure *that* is passed around."

"You got it." Lincoln didn't question Marcus' orders, and it wasn't long before his friend completed the task.

"You should understand something about—" Jennifer's sentence ended in a high-pitched squeal and he imagined his best friend carting off the lioness.

The moment not another soul lingered, Marcus dug his fingers into her silken fur. Her rolling purr intensified, vibrating through him and his lion was quick to return the sounds. Satisfaction and serenity unlike he'd ever known thrummed through his veins. He had her. *Her*. His one and only mate. Despite interference, he had her. And he wouldn't let go.

He rubbed his hands over her ears, tracing the lines of her taut neck, massaging the tense muscles of her shoulders, and finally following her legs to her massive paws. Strong and deadly, fierce and protective. He retraced his path until he was able to cup her massive head, and he encouraged her to turn her beautiful gaze to him.

When her eyes clashed with his, he spoke, "Are you going to shift for me? Let me get my hands on your curvy body once again. I want nothing but to taste and claim you until we're too exhausted to move. But I can't do that unless you change for me." He stroked her whiskers brushing them back and then he traced her nose with a single finger, smiling when she chuffed in pleasure. "Let me mate you, Penelope. And then," he tilted his head to the side, exposing his neck, "you can make me yours."

It wasn't something alphas generally allowed, being that vulnerable was hard for the average dominant male, but Marcus was anything but average. He was strong enough to know that mating went both ways, and he couldn't be fully tied to his mate unless she sank her teeth into his flesh in return. His lion roared in approval, and now he simply had to wait for Penelope's response.

By the time the last syllable left his lips, her change was upon her. A body-shaking tremor enveloped her, and the first crack of bone signaled her change. But that was all the warning he got. Like him, her own transition was fierce and had he blinked he would've missed her shift from lion the human. The stronger the beast, the quicker the change. It had always been this way. It was part of how an alpha was determined. A male couldn't lead a pride if he wasn't ready and strong enough to defend it. In many cases, a rapid shift was the decision between seeing the dawn of a new day and being planted six feet under.

It was only right that the mate of the strongest alpha on the continent was more than a match for him.

Suddenly his arms were filled with a woman covered in plump curves and the sweetest scent he'd ever encountered. Her musk filled the air, her moans enveloping him, and her groans tormented his lion.

Before she could say a word, he cupped her face and brought her mouth to his. Despite being beneath her, he took control of their kiss. It was frenzied and fierce, their tongues fighting for dominance as they tasted each other's flavors. Sweet. He knew the same word kept rolling through his mind, but he couldn't think of any other way to describe her. Just… Sweet. Wait. No. He had another word.

His.

And if he wasn't careful, he'd claim her on the front porch, bits of old and dry wood digging into his flesh. Or worse, her flesh. No, that couldn't happen. His first responsibility was no longer the lions of the continent, but the single, delicious female. He fought to gentle their kiss, lessened the passion to a low simmer instead of this rolling uncontrollable boil, but he had to accept their passion had only two settings at the moment: on and… Okay, just on. He forced himself to tear his mouth from hers, his grip keeping her from re-initiating the connection.

Penelope whimpered and whined but Marcus was not giving in. "I'm not claiming you on a fucking porch. Where else can we go? Inside the house? Who does it belong to?"

Not that he really cared. If it held a bed, it now belonged to him and that was that.

Except, her next sound wasn't one of desire or need from him, but of distress.

"Penelope?"

She opened her eyes, exposing the startling gold of her lioness, and whimpered once again. "Marcus," she whined, "I don't want to go in there."

The expression that flitted across her face, the sadness in her gaze, was enough to bank his arousal. Having a mate wasn't just about sex and claiming, it was so much more. "What is it about this place, sweetheart? Whose is it?" She tried to tear her attention from him, but he refused to let her hide herself. "Sweetheart?"

He wasn't sure if she would answer, had no idea if she'd deny him, and he mentally breathed a sigh of relief when she finally replied, "Mine. It's my house, but I haven't lived here since I was eighteen and it came to me when my parents died."

His heart hurt for her, tightened and the beat stuttered as he viewed the pain in her expression. "Did they pass here? It that why it's so painful? Palmer said this was Georgie's land…"

"No," she shook her head. "It's mine, but Georgie is a cousin, which is why they could tie her here." Marcus sensed there was more, and he bit his tongue, waiting for her to speak again. "The house doesn't hold any fond memories for me, so the first moment I could, I left. Everything is as it was when they passed away, and I pay someone to come in occasionally to clean, but otherwise I haven't crossed the threshold in eight years."

"So, we'll go somewhere else," he brushed a strand of hair that lingered on her cheek and tucked it behind her ear. "Wherever you want to go."

"We can…" She licked her lips, and he swallowed the groan that threatened to burst from his chest. Her mouth was so damned tempting.

"Penelope?"

"They hated me. The town doesn't like me, but they wouldn't be so bad if my parents had supported me. Except they didn't so…"

Marcus swallowed the growl that threated to vault past his lips. "You're perfect. *Perfect.*" He tugged her down so he could brush a soft kiss across her lips. "We'll find somewhere else. We'll go to a hotel. There has to be one around here somewhere, right?" She opened her mouth to speak and he shook his head. "No, I won't have you uncomfortable or surrounded by bad memories."

She nibbled her lower lip, taunting him with the action. "No, we can mate here. We can banish the bad memories, can't we?"

"With you, sweetheart, we'll make nothing but good memories. We'll make this house our own."

With her blinding smile, Marcus was more than happy to do just that.

In a flurry of movement, he found himself on his feet, Penelope in his arms as he broke through the front door. He clutched her to his chest, and smiled widely at her squeal when he bolted up the stairs. She was right, the home was clean and tidy, not a speck of dust tickling his nose as he strode down the hall.

"Which one was yours?"

"Last door on the left." She pointed at the single door that remained ajar.

When they entered, he strode straight to the bed and placed her on the soft surface, following her down and blanketing her with his body. "Is this where you dreamed of finding your mate?" At her nod, he continued. "Then making you mine here is perfect."

CHAPTER THREE

And it was perfect. Her perfect pale skin was bared to his gaze and air whooshed from his lungs when he was struck with awe. She was his. Every luscious, curvaceous inch visible belonged to him.

He skimmed her smooth skin with his palm, memorizing the rise and fall, the dip and curve, of her body. When he stroked her side, she trembled, and when he cupped her breast, she whimpered. The white plump mounds were tipped with hard, colored nipples that begged for his mouth.

"Marcus..." she said his name with a breathy moan.

She almost stole his control with that single whisper, and he kept the animal at bay using every ounce of strength he possessed. He could get through this without embarrassing himself, without rushing her, if she wouldn't talk. Or move. Or breathe, because when she exhaled, she blew even more of her delicious scent into him. The woman was a walking talking trembling threat to his control.

"Marcus…"

Dammit if she didn't quiet, things would be over before they began. Already he was aching and throbbing for her. Already? It had been that way from the moment he spied her in the library. Now it was simply magnified by a million. Because he had her in his arms, and no one to stop him. He may have been under a spell when he chased her scent across the continent, but there was no denying she was his mate.

When she opened her mouth again, he realized he needed to keep those lips busy. Not that it was a hardship.

He pressed his mouth to hers, drinking in her flavors as he slid his tongue past her lips. She rocked against him, trembling and riding, pressing her body against his, harder than before. And as their tongues dueled, he let his touch wander. He petted and stroked every inch he could reach and growled when

Penelope did the same. She clawed and scratched at his shoulders, gripped his upper arms, and dug her fingers into his forearms as she fought to make him touch her where she desired.

Marcus chuckled, easing from their kiss for a moment. Just long enough to murmur a handful of words. "You're mating an alpha, sweetheart. I'll touch you wherever I want when I'm good and ready."

"Can you be ready to touch me here?" *Here* happened to be her left breast. "Or kiss me there?"

His mouth watered with the suggestion, and his beast roared in satisfaction. Her lioness might not be able to take him in a fight, but her quiet pleas and words that held no hint of faltering proved she was a match for him in the bedroom.

"Coincidentally, that's what I want too."

He didn't hesitate to capture the single nub with his lips, to flick it with his tongue. He smiled against her flesh when she gripped his head and pricked his scalp with her small claws. As he focused on the small bit of flesh, he continued to stroke her body. All the while, she writhed beneath him, pleading, whining, and begging for more.

She was dangerous. Those small sounds and tiny syllables threatening to undo him before he slid into her body. But he refused to pop off like an adolescent cub. This was their mating, and he was going to do it properly. They only had one chance to get it right.

Eventually he abandoned her left breast, and continued his travels over her body. Damn, he wasn't sure what he'd done to deserve her, but he was going to take and keep her. She was made for him. One hundred percent for him. He kissed and nibbled his way between her breasts, continued his path over the gentle rounding of her stomach, and didn't stop his travels until he was on his stomach between her plump spread thighs.

Heaven. Her musk called to him, and the moist pinkness exposed to his gaze beckoned him. She was gorgeous, flush and ready for his possession. His mouth watered and he took what he desired. He placed a soft kiss to her inner thigh followed by a gentle scrape of his fangs over the sensitive skin and was gratified at her desperate shout.

"Marcus!"

He smiled against her skin and rubbed his cheek along her inner thigh. "Right here."

"Marcus," she pleaded.

"Tell me what you need." He snared her gaze with his own. "Tell me."

"You. Just you."

She wanted him? She'd have him. Just as soon as he tasted her.

Which he did; he lapped at the seam of her sex lips, licking and tasting, swallowing the proof of her arousal, and suckling her clit.

He memorized every twitch, cataloged every tremble, and gloried in every needy whine and he resolved to repeat them until she screamed his name. The moment she balanced on that precipice, he'd take her. Take her and make her his.

*

Penelope wanted to be his. She wanted him to take her and make her his. Then again, when he sucked on her clit and sent those delicious tingles down her spine, she figured this was kind of okay too.

She rocked against his mouth, taking from him as she fought to reach her pinnacle. It was there, so close and yet still out of reach. But sometimes, the journey could be better than the arrival. Because right now, the journey was really, really fucking good.

Then he made it better; his blunt fingertips circled her opening, and two digits slid deeply into her. He stretched her and filled her, stroking with his talented fingers. That added sensation had her nearer to the edge, shoving her to the very precipice and she knew it wouldn't take much more to send her tumbling over.

She rolled her body, riding his tongue and fucking herself on his fingers as she fought for more. But it wasn't his touch, it wasn't his mouth or tongue, or even his heat that sent her flying.

It was his eyes. The way his gaze poured into her, the way it begged for her, the way it branded her with his possession and not just asked—but demanded—her surrender. She was powerless beneath his silent domination, unable to stop her lioness' immediate response to her mate's wordless demand. He wanted her to come, and she was unable to stop it.

The pleasure gradually building bubbled over and consumed her in a blinding wave. Her heat contracted around him, milking him, and she couldn't wait until it was his length deep within her. Bliss enveloped her from head to toe, plucking at her nerves and sending joy pouring through her veins. Her body was no longer her own, muscles trembling and spasming uncontrollably. Her toes curled and she was unable to stop her legs when they wrapped around him.

Her shout of completion echoed off the bedroom walls and was joined by a satisfied growl from Marcus.

Penelope's orgasm continued, the sensations never ending, and if the foreplay was this good, she'd simply die when he finally claimed her.

"Please, please, please… I need you." Her lion was whining and chuffing, begging Penelope to move things along. Both parts of her ached to belong to him, and it needed to happen already. "Make me yours."

With a snarl, Marcus abandoned the juncture of her thighs and left her long enough to tear his clothes to shreds and leave them in a pile on the floor. Then he was back, climbing up her body and anticipation thrummed through her veins. His gaze remained focused on her, never wavering as he levered himself above her. A shift of his hips, and then the blunted tip of his shaft pressed against her very center. In one great heave, he speared her with his length, and a roar escaped him at that same moment. "Mine!"

Yes, yes she was his.

He stretched her, sending a tendril of pain through her blood, and it twined around the pleasure still pulsing through her. That sting merely encouraged her release to continue, the pleasure overwhelming until she could hardly breathe.

He withdrew slightly, his thickness caressing her inner walls, and then he shoved forward in a fierce thrust once again. "Mine."

She wrapped her legs around his hips, holding him close. "Yours."

He repeated the move, a slight retreat and then a forceful lunge. "Forever mine."

"Yes," she gasped.

Then words were beyond her. She was unable to catch her breath, unable to think beyond the pleasure and need that consumed her. Their bodies writhed in a dance as old as time, hips meeting, skin sliding against skin, and their breaths mingling as his mouth hovered above her.

The sounds of their sex filled the air while the scent of their combined musk soaked into their pores and coated them. No, it wasn't just sex, it was pure, animalistic mating. Lion to lioness, man to woman, forever.

"Come for me." He gave another fierce thrust, slamming the bed against the wall. "Come for me, and then I'll claim you." Another thrust and retreat. "Make you mine."

Penelope did as he asked, taking the pleasure of his body and gathering it to herself. The rest of her orgasm had not drifted far, and his words sent it rushing forward once again. Only this time, it was stronger, overwhelming in its intensity and she cried out as it crashed through her blood. "Oh God!"

"Now, Penelope. Now. I want you to be mine."

She couldn't deny him, and this time her scream ended with a mighty roar. Her lion leapt forward, forcing her human teeth to become sharp fangs, the tips easily able to sink into Marcus' flesh. And then she did.

She struck, pressing them through his skin and into the muscle, taking him for herself. Her next yell was muffled against his flesh as he did the same to her. It was no longer simply the combined scents of their sweat and musk, but also the coppery tang of their blood that surrounded them.

The shifter born magic that lived inside them reached for the other; his stretching and twining with hers while hers beckoned him. As their release thundered through their bodies, the ethereal lines wrapped around each other and tied the two spirits together. Yes, sharing their bodies was an integral part of a mating, but this soul deep connection would knot them together until the end of time.

And as the lines solidified in their connection, her beast was soothed by Marcus' presence. Because it was done, they were mated, and there wasn't a damn thing anyone could do. Her pride may not view her as a worthy lioness, but fuck them.

Marcus was hers. *Hers.* And if they didn't like it, she'd have her mate kick their asses.

His shaft swelled and stretched her further, locking them together in the final moments of their binding. His thickness wouldn't allow him to retreat as soon as his orgasm ended; they would be joined together in a closeness only shared by mates.

A new heat filled her, the warmth of his cum coating her inner walls. His pure essence would alter her true scent, adding a bit of his to her own. One and all would know she belonged to him. In return, she knew her bite on his shoulder would do the same. Maybe not to the extent of the alteration of hers, but the bitches better watch out because she would straight up cut them if they went near her mate.

Marcus trembled, his big frame shaking and the vibrations transferred to her, sending another spear of pleasure down her spine. It wasn't until he withdrew his fangs from her flesh that she realized the motions were due to chuckles and not emotions that overwhelmed him.

At his retreat, she withdrew her own, and lapped at the wound she caused. It was big and would definitely be visible to everyone. Good. That part of her mind settled, she returned her attention to her laughing mate. "What's so funny?"

"You." He still remained tied to her, his length hard and firm within her, and he propped himself on his elbows. "You're going to 'straight up cut them'?"

Oh. She forgot he could read her mind. Dammit.

"Well, you're my mate. You're not the only one who gets to be a possessive asshole, you know."

He lapped at her lips, and she opened to him, tasting her blood in his mouth an instant before he retreated. "I didn't say I didn't like it. It just surprised me. To think the woman I hunted down, the prissy perfect librarian is violent at heart… Makes me hard."

Penelope rolled her eyes. "A stiff wind would make you hard."

"Maybe when I was an adolescent cub, but now..." He slid his arms beneath her, and suddenly she was astride him, her legs straddling his hips while his shaft was still deep within her. "It's all about you."

"Oh."

"Exactly." He rubbed her hips and then cupped her ass, kneading the mounds. "Now, let's see how long I can stay hard."

Penelope definitely liked the sound of that idea.

CHAPTER FOUR

The next morning, Penelope rubbed her nose against Marcus' bare chest, inhaling his musky scent and savoring his closeness. He stroked her with those large, callused palms and she remembered how gentle they could be. And how wicked.

"So, you're kind of a big deal?" she murmured against him. They'd have to talk about the furry elephant in the room at some point.

Marcus merely chuckled, his body trembling with the sound. "You could say that. But I only want to be important to one person." He cupped her cheeks, encouraging her to tilt her head back and meet his gaze. "You."

Aww, if he kept saying sweet things like that, she was a goner. "Well, you're kind of a big deal to me."

He lowered his head, and she stretched toward him, until their lips met in a gentle kiss. It was completely opposite of the passionate meetings that had consumed them the last twenty-four hours. Now, their lions were able to enjoy a little sweetness rather than the fiery need of mating. He withdrew from her, a small smile hovering between them as he relaxed against the bed.

She propped her chin on his chest, staring at the man she'd spend the rest of her life with. She wasn't sure how she got so lucky. Going from hardly wanted, barely tolerated, to being claimed was a novel experience. And there was no doubt Marcus wanted her. No, it was more than want. She wouldn't be able to live without him and had no doubt he felt the same.

"What you looking at?" He whispered the words.

"You." She pressed a kiss to his chest, the soft gold fur that seemed to permanently grace his skin brushing her nose. "Just you."

"And what do you think about me?"

A blush heated Penelope's cheeks, burning her face, and she squirmed against him. What could she tell him? That she didn't think she'd ever be able to live without him? That she couldn't wait to have his cubs? That if he so much as looked at another female she would cut the bitch and claw out the woman's eyes? God, he'd turned her into a violence craving homicidal bitch.

"Penny?"

"You know what I think about you," she grumbled. "I yelled it often enough, didn't I?"

Another chuckle from Marcus. "Yeah, you did. I like making you yell. I like making you scream my name." He stroked her back, fingertips scraping her delicate skin. "Want me to do it again?"

Penelope hurt in places she didn't even know existed, and she wasn't sure she could survive another round. At least not until she got some food in her stomach.

She shook her head. "Feed me first."

"Food is more important than me claiming you again?" His tone held a hint of annoyance and she almost rushed to deny his statement, but a girl had to keep her guy on his toes.

"*Good* food…"

Marcus mock growled, and flipped their positions, rolling until Penelope was pinned beneath his large bulk. He blanketed her like a seductive cloth, sending a sliver of arousal through her body. It took that single brush, that slide of skin on skin, and she was ready for him once again. The yellow of his eyes and the rumble of his chest with a deep purr told Penelope he felt the same.

But then her stomach growled and the burgeoning desire quickly vanished.

"Food." He rolled from her, quickly gained his feet beside the bed, and held out his hand. "Come on, let's eat."

Penelope allowed herself to be drawn from the comfort of their small nest and went easily into the circle of his arms. She didn't bother protesting when he swung her up into his embrace. "You know, I doubt there's any food in the house."

"Don't worry, Lincoln took care of things around three this morning. There's enough here to feed five average full grown lions."

"Well, that should last us a couple days," she murmured as she clung to him when he tromped down the stairs.

Marcus grinned down at her and didn't break his stride. "Sweetheart, that's just for me and it *might* last the rest of the day."

"Uh-huh. And you let Lincoln in here? I thought big bad alpha lions were super protective of their mates. What's up with that?"

He padded into the kitchen and placed her on the old wooden table. She squeaked as her bare flesh collided with the cool surface and she opened her mouth to yell at him, but his voice cut her off.

"You're covered in my scent. You've got my mark on your shoulder, and evidence of our mating coating your skin. There is no way he wouldn't know." He leaned forward and nibbled her lower lip. "And I trust Lincoln with my life. Besides, he was the only one with balls big enough to step onto the property. The other guys are good but they're..."

"Pussies. The word you're looking for is pussies."

"*Woman.*"

Penelope ignored him. "So, it seems it's good to be a big deal. I think I could get used to this kind of treatment."

"This kind of treatment…" His gaze was intent on her, his eyes seeming to search for something, but she wasn't sure what he was looking for. "Could you get used to it somewhere else?"

Wow. From teasing to heavy in an instant. She met his serious stare. "Define somewhere else."

A look of vulnerability coated his features, and she figured she was the only person who'd ever seen the alpha unsure. "You know where the North American headquarters are, and I also travel when needed."

The question was there, even if the words didn't leave his mouth. He wanted to know if she'd moved with him, if she'd leave her life behind and follow him.

She cupped his face, rubbing her thumbs along his cheekbones and stared deeply into his eyes. "I've lived here my whole life and I hate the people here. The town, the surrounding land is gorgeous, but the pride despises me." She ignored his rolling growl. "Home isn't a place, Marcus. For me, home is you. Just you."

With those words, any thoughts of food were discarded. Especially when he claimed her on the kitchen table, and then the counter, and then there was the hallway as they tried to make it back upstairs…

But when all was said and done, Penelope was well and truly claimed and looking forward to spending the rest of her life with Marcus. Whether that be in a nowhere town like Ryland, or beneath the bright lights of the city, she'd always be at home… With Marcus.

THE END

If you enjoyed this book, please be totally awesomesauce and leave a review so others may discover it as well. Long review or short, your opinion will help other readers make future purchasing decisions. So, go forth and rate my level-o-awesome!

By the way… below is a list of the books in the Quick & Furry series:

Quick & Furry #1: Chasing Tail
Quick & Furry #2: Tailing Her
Quick & Furry #3: On Her Tail
Quick & Furry #4: Heads or Tails

ABOUT THE AUTHOR

Ex-dance teacher, former accountant and erstwhile collectible doll salesperson, New York Times and USA Today bestselling author Celia Kyle now writes paranormal romances for readers who:

1) Like super hunky heroes (they generally get furry)
2) Dig beautiful women (who have a few more curves than the average lady)
3) Love laughing in (and out of) bed.

It goes without saying that there's always a happily-ever-after for her characters, even if there are a few road bumps along the way.

Today she lives in Central Florida and writes full-time with the support of her loving husband and two finicky cats.

If you'd like to be notified of new releases, special sales, and get FREE eBooks, subscribe here: http://celiakyle.com/news

You can find Celia online at:

http://celiakyle.com
http://facebook.com/authorceliakyle
http://twitter.com/celiakyle

COPYRIGHT

Made in the USA
Monee, IL
21 January 2020